Little Li
for Little People

Victoria Dimmock

BookLeaf
Publishing
India | USA | UK

Little Life Lessons for Little People © 2023
Victoria Dimmock

All rights reserved.

Presentation by *BookLeaf Publishing*

Web: www.bookleafpub.com

E-mail: info@bookleafpub.com

ISBN: 9789358738186

First edition 2023

To the children in my family who bring joy to everyone they meet.

ACKNOWLEDGEMENT

Thank you to my husband Charlie for your support and encouragement, and thank you to my family. You all mean the world to me.

Thank you to my daughter, Faith, who provided the beautiful artwork for the front cover.

PREFACE

A collection of poems for children about important life lessons.

True

"What are your plans for today, True?"
Mum asked, moving boxes about,
"I'll probably just laze around all day,
Or see if anyone wants to hang out."

"Or you could help at the soup kitchen, love,
They always need help in there."
"I'd rather not. No thanks," True scoffed,
Ignoring her mum's steely stare.

In the car, on the way, she huffed and sighed,
Her afternoon was going to pot,
She wanted to meet up with friends today,
Not pour soup for this sorry lot.

The first man she served was tired and weary,
His beard was tangled and grey,
He smiled his thanks as he took the bowl,
And shuffled shyly away.

The next was a woman much younger than her
mother,
Although her face looked worn and sad,
True smiled at the woman with tears in her eyes,
Her earlier thoughts made her feel bad.

How could she be so spoilt when people were
living like this?
She had everything she would ever need,
As a little boy made his way over to the table,
True hated herself for her greed.

His face was dirty but he smiled away,
True couldn't take it anymore,
She walked around and gave the boy a cuddle,
His bare feet cold on the floor.

She apologised to her mum and promised to help
again,
Her eyes had been opened that day,
Everywhere in the world, there are people less
fortunate than you,
And poverty will never just go away.

If we all lend a hand and give up our time,
We could make the world a better place,
If we look out for one another when we can,
We will be a stronger and better human race.

Frankie

BANG! BANG! BANG! Olivia covered her ears,
And Mummy said, "Not again!"
Whir! Whir! Saw! Saw! Came from the shed,
And it was only 7am.

Frankie had his goggles on,
Tools were all over the floor,
"It's too early for all that, love."
Mum's tone was too cross to ignore.

"Sorry, mum. I'm almost done.
Just one more coat of paint."
As he revealed his newest project,
A dolls house; intricate and quaint.

Olivia "oohed" and went to touch,
But Frankie held her back,
"Liv, this isn't for you. Get out!"
As Mum gave him a whack.

"Don't be mean to your sister!"
"But I've worked non stop.
I could win first prize, you know!
I can't risk it being dropped."

Mum rolled her eyes and took Liv upstairs,
And Frankie carried on,
The house was close to perfection,
His chance of winning was strong.

Finally! After hours on end,
The house was up to scratch,
He couldn't wait to present his work,
The others had met their match.

The competition was a success,
Frankie beat them all,
He now had one thing left to do,
and he went running down the hall.

"Surprise, Liv! Happy birthday!"
His sister beamed with joy,
"It was always going to be yours in the end,
"It's not just to look at. It's a toy!"

"Just make sure to take good care."
Olivia excitedly agreed,
His mum had never been more proud,
Than of Frankie's lovely good deed

Imogen

Starting secondary school is a tough, tough time,
But Imogen was excited,
She couldn't wait to make new friends,
Despite her peers being divided.

She already knew Holly but not that well,
They ran in different circles,
Holly wore glasses and had braces too,
Which in itself created some hurdles.

In Teen World, you had to look a certain way,
Else you wouldn't make the cut,
If you didn't fall into their "perfect image",
You might find yourself in a rut.

But Imogen didn't let this idiocy faze her,
She believed that beauty lies within,
So when it came to choosing friends,
She was always going to win.

On her very first day, she saw firsthand,
How evil some girls could be,
A group picked out Holly straight away,
And taunted her ruthlessly.

At first, Imogen couldn't believe her eyes,
She didn't know where to look,
Should she get her phone out like the other kids,
Or keep her nose in her book?

But the other kids were laughing now,
As Holly tried not to cry,
Imogen felt her anger boil over,
She couldn't just stand by.

"If you pick on her, you pick on me too",
Imogen loudly proclaimed,
The nasty girl scoffed and Imogen said,
"All of you should be ashamed!"

They walked away from the adolescent crowd,
And Imogen led the way,
Holding her friends arm she spoke,
"I've got your back, okay?"

"Be the shepherd, not the sheep"
"That's what my Grandma taught me,
And Holly smiled through tears of joy,
"And no one wants a friend like Courtney".

The girls giggled at their triumphant friendship,
As Grandma's advice rang true,
If you are there for the little person,
One day they might be there for you.

Faith

Faith had decided this year would be different,
She was going to try something new,
She needed to find who she was inside,
Her personality was waiting to break through.

Could she get in with the popular kids?
They were all so pretty and pristine,
They wore make up and styled their hair every day,
Although they were actually quite mean.

There was always drama amongst those girls,
Fighting over who's boyfriend was who's,
They didn't do very well in class,
And Faith heard that they smoked in the loos.

"Maybe not", Faith thought. "I like being smart".
Maybe the chess club instead,
These guys are all methodical thinkers,
And it's surely the best way to get ahead.

But alas, they were too clever by far,
Faith knew she couldn't compete,
She didn't know how to play chess anyway,

And she wasn't even sure she could cheat.

"Try again", Faith said with some hope this
time,
She could always join a band,
She played a few tunes on the ukulele,
With a guitar, she'd be a dab hand.

They looked so cool and played rock and roll,
But she didn't really want to sing,
She didn't want to have to dye her hair,
And she wouldn't suit an eyebrow ring.

The writers were too fantastical,
The artists were too deep,
The math whizzes were too boring,
And the fan girls were nothing but sheep.

Faith thought for a moment before it hit her,
She didn't have to actually change,
She just had to be true to herself,
She was quirky and sometimes a bit strange.

And that was ok because she was happy that
way,
And the misfits were her tribe,
She didn't need to look elsewhere,
They shared a certain vibe.

So you really shouldn't have to force it,
Your personality will find its way,
It's the unique thing about us all,
And no one can ever take that away.

Ella

"I just can't get it right!" Ella shouted, upset.
She threw the pencil to the floor,
Then she grabbed the paper and tore it up,
And shouted a little bit more.

"What's all the fuss?" Her father asked,
"Do you want me to give it a try?"
Ella stomped her feet and shook her head,
And let out a frustrated sigh.

She began to get ready as she was late for
school,
But her hair just wouldn't sit right,
She growled and pouted and huffed and puffed,
As she tried with all her might.

"Can I give it a go?" Her mother asked,
But Ella just got irate,
"I can't do anything! And I've had enough!"
She couldn't even get her tie on straight.

She dropped to the floor and cried and cried,
Her emotions were weighing her down,
"I can't do this anymore. I've tried so hard!"
"But I feel like I'm going to drown!"

In came Lilly who sat quietly beside her,
And began to brush Ella's hair,
She softly hushed her big sister's tears,
And whispered to her, "There, there".

"It's ok to ask for help sometimes, you know",
"You don't have to struggle alone",
"We all feel angry and annoyed and that's ok",
"But you're never on your own".

Ella knew her little sister was right,
But emotions are such big things,
It's hard to explain what you're feeling at times,
The tidal wave the emotion brings.

Never be afraid to ask for help,
Guidance is what we all need,
No matter your age or who you are,
You never have to concede.

A problem shared is a problem halved,
And it makes the burden less,
If you just open up and let it out,
It can help to relive all the stress.

Ella nodded too upset to talk,
But Lilly smiled and said,
"You have me to support you always",
As she kissed her sisters head.

Lilly

"Everybody find a partner,"
The teacher told the class,
So Lilly looked around to see,
Who she was going to ask.

The new girl sat alone in the corner,
So Lilly made her way,
Over to the girl with the worried stare,
Her name was Georgia-May.

"Can we work together?" Lilly smiled,
Georgia-May turned around,
There was no one behind her or anywhere near,
And Lilly had already sat down.

"You really want to work with me?"
Georgia-May was unsure,
Lilly laughed and shrugged her shoulders,
"Have you not been asked before?"

Georgia-May recoiled and looked away,
Other kids normally stared,
They didn't know how to act around her,
They might even be a little bit scared.

Scared of the unknown, unfortunately so,

But, with Lilly, this wasn't the case,
She wasn't put off by rumours,
Or the difference in her new friends face.

"Why wouldn't other kids want to work with you?"
Lilly just couldn't see,
"It's because I'm different. Nothing else.
It's easier to ignore me."

Lilly was puzzled and still confused,
She wasn't sure what to do,
Did the others know something she didn't?
"What exactly is different about you?"

Georgia-May chuckled and grabbed her hand,
"I have Down's syndrome, silly!"
And as the concern turned to relief,
"Is that it?" Cried Lilly.

"I thought it was something really bad,
But I'm so so glad it's not!"
Georgia-May felt at ease, at last,
"I also giggle a lot."

Lilly cuddled her brand new friend,
"Then you are just like me,
We can be giggly and different together,
Just like everyone else should be."

Elsie & Mimi

"Oh no!!!" Cried Elsie at the top of her lungs,
Her picture had been destroyed,
The one she had spent all afternoon painting,
She stomped from her room, so annoyed.

She marched into the kitchen and showed her
mum,
Her tears were falling now,
"It's completely ruined!" She sobbed and
sobbed,
"But I just don't understand how!"

The picture was wet and the paint had all run,
As Elsie realised in vain,
She must have left her window open,
She didn't think it would rain.

Mummy cuddled Elsie and hushed her quiet,
Her hearty sobs filled the air,
But sitting on the stairs was her sister, Mimi,
Wearing a look of despair.

Mimi had snuck into Elsie's room,
Earlier that day,
She'd knocked over a cup of water,

And then she'd run away.

The guilt was overwhelming her,
She'd made her sister sad,
She had to tell Elsie what really happened,
But Elsie would then be mad.

Mummy always said to them both,
Be honest and don't tell lies,
Lying will make it much much worse,
And Mummy's are often wise.

So Mimi took her sisters hand,
"I have something to tell you,
It was an accident but it's all my fault,
I was touching things I wasn't supposed to."

Mummy held her breath as Elsie,
Thought for a little while,
Then she hugged her sister tight,
Which made her mummy smile.

"Thank you. I thought it was really me,
I'm glad I wasn't to blame,
I'm angry that you went in my room,
But you were honest just the same."

"I forgive you but on one condition,
We have to fix it please,"

Mimi agreed to make things right,
And they worked together with ease.

The painting looked better than it did before,
The twins were a right happy pair,
And Mummy stuck it straight on the wall,
"No more accidents up there!"

Willow

"For my birthday this year, I'd like a toolbox,"
Willow announced to her dad,
"Wouldn't you prefer a doll instead?
A toolbox is a toy for a lad!"

"Mum, can I please have a toolbox? Please?"
But Mum was not so sure,
"How about some ponies or barbies instead?
What do you want a toolbox for?"

"Please will you buy me a toolbox, Aunty
Sammy?"
Her face was hopeful and still,
"I've already got you some arts and craft stuff,
You can't paint with a hammer and drill."

"It's almost your birthday, Willow. Are you
excited?"
Her grandma beamed with joy,
"I only want a toolbox please,
I don't want any other toy."

"Everyone keeps asking me,
And I want a toolbox of my own,
No one seems to be listening"

So she went and sat all alone.

Grandma spoke to Grandad Bob,
They knew just what to do,
And on her birthday, the surprise they brought,
Willow's smile quickly grew.

Just for her! Her very own toolbox,
Now she could fix her toys,
She wouldn't have to wait for an adult,
And toolboxes aren't just for boys.

Grandad had another surprise hidden behind his
back,
He'd brought his toolbox too,
He promised to teach her what each tool was for,
And the difference between a nut and a screw.

Willow was over the moon with delight,
As her grandfather led the way,
All it took was some encouragement,
And they'd made their granddaughter's day.

Eliza

On her way home from school one day,
Eliza stopped by the lake,
"I wonder if we will see any mermaids,
Taking a sunbathing break."

Alyssia giggled and shook her head,
"Mermaids only live in the sea,"
But Eliza was certain she'd seen one before,
At least her mum had agreed.

They continued down towards the park,
And came across some mushroom rings,
"Don't step inside them," Eliza warned,
"Those fairies are pesky things."

Alyssia looked confused at this,
As Eliza began to explain,
"You could be punished for disturbing their
dance,"
"No, you've got it wrong again!"

Eliza was feeling a little disheartened,
Surely her friend was wrong,
Her mum had told her all the stories,
And she had believed them for so long.

"Alyssia says I'm wrong about fairies!"
She cried to her mum,
"And there aren't any mermaids in the lake,
I'm feeling really dumb."

"Don't be silly," mummy said,
"Alyssia just believes different things,
Maybe she's only seen mermaids at sea,
And she doesn't know about fairy rings."

"It's ok to have different opinions,
Just respect each others' belief,"
And Eliza smiled warmly,
Well, that was a relief.

The next day, Alyssia showed Eliza,
A picture she'd made in class,
"It's my beautiful pet unicorn,
She eats daffodils and grass."

Eliza had never seen a unicorn,
But she believed that her best friend had,
So she said "What a wonderful pet you have!"
Since believing in unicorns could never be bad.

Franklin

Franklin and his cousins were all getting cars for
Christmas,
The red and yellow Little Tikes,
They were all so excited to get their gifts,
Cars were so much better than bikes.

Albert couldn't wait to drive his car fast,
Speeding down the road he would go,
He'd be faster than the old lady on her scooter,
No one would ever call him slow.

Edward wanted to carry his toys around with
him,
He would give them all a ride,
He'd drive very carefully from A to B,
And have his favourite bear by his side.

Amiya wanted to show her friends her new car,
It would be all shiny and new,
Her nursery friends would all be jealous,
They'd want to have one too.

On Christmas morning they all awoke,
And ran downstairs to see,
All four cars were perfectly placed,

Next to the Christmas tree.

Albert, Edward and Amiya,
Jumped inside their cars with glee,
But Franklin pushed his car over,
And got down on his hands and knees.

He pulled over his tools and started fixing,
An imaginary problem with the car,
The parents looked at him in awe,
He tightened the wheels like a star.

Franklin didn't want to drive his car,
He was happy just to repair,
He loved to find out just how things worked,
And a good mechanic was rare.

His dad pulled him in for a massive hug,
"I'm really proud of you, son,"
Franklin just smiled and hugged him back,
"Fixing things is really fun!"

Kaleb

In a certain school or so they say,
There's a boy who's oh so strong,
He can lift bookcases over his head,
And pull a bus along.

He picks up benches with kids on top,
And throws frisbees really far,
He can climb a tree all the way to the top,
And stop a moving car.

But his classmates don't understand him,
They are scared by his strength,
They think that Kaleb might hurt them,
And avoid him at great length.

This makes Kaleb incredibly sad,
All he wanted was a friend,
He tried to talk to the other kids,
But they just couldn't comprehend.

So one sunny day, Kaleb sat alone,
Eating his lunch on a bench,
Watching his classmates playing together,
It made his heart wrench.

Until he heard screams and alarm bells wailing,
Cries for help could be heard,
The building his classroom was in was on fire,
He ran over without saying a word.

He saw the kids who had been mean to him,
Who had teased and called him names,
He saw them trapped and scared inside,
The fire surrounding the doorframes.

Kaleb plucked up every ounce of his strength,
And smashed at the building's wall,
Eventually, brick by brick fell away,
Until he had freed them all.

His classmates were eternally grateful,
And friends they all became,
And Kaleb was the school hero,
And was never picked on again!

Grace

When Grace is poorly and feeling sick,
Mummy is always there,
She gives Grace soup and medicine,
And softly brushes her hair.

When Grace is sad and feeling low,
Mummy's arms open wide,
To give out hugs and a listening ear,
And she's always on Grace's side.

When Grace is tired and needs to sleep,
Mummy's patient and calm,
She tells Grace stories and sings her songs,
And shelters her from harm.

But now Mummy is poorly and feeling down,
So before she gets any worse,
Grace has decided to be there for Mum,
And be her personal nurse.

She brings Mummy water and holds her hand,
And gives her cuddles too,
She helps with housework and tidying up,
And makes her feel brand new.

If Mummy's ever feeling upset,
There's one thing that's guaranteed,
Grace can always cheer her up,
And knows just what Mummy needs.

It's always good to help out Mum,
She works so very hard,
To make sure Grace is always smiling,
And remains her little star.

So when Mum needs a helping hand,
Grace is there on call,
And Mummy's there when Grace needs her,
They help each other through it all.

Anna

One day, Anna was playing in the bath,
And spotted a bottle up high,
It was shiny and pretty and not meant for
children,
A bottle of mum's hair dye.

Anna knew it was put out of her reach,
But she was determined to knock it down,
She threw all her toys at the dye, one by one,
And eventually, it tumbled to the ground.

In her hand she held the forbidden dye,
And much to her surprise,
It wasn't brown or red or blonde,
It was called Pink Sunrise!

Anna poured the mixture generously onto,
Her hair and worked it in deep,
Her mum would be mad but the next day at
school,
Her classmates would flock to her like sheep.

As she walked through the school gates pink
locks flowing,
Everyone stopped to stare,

They all wanted to know what had happened,
To the girl with the super pink hair.

Maybe a fairy had come in the night,
And blessed her with one wish,
She'd asked for glorious, magnificent hair,
So the fairy gave her wand a swish.

Maybe her hair had magical powers,
Maybe her hair could heal,
It had to be special with that sort of colour,
They needed to know for real.

But Anna just turned and flicked her hair,
And she swore never to tell,
The secret of how her former blonde waves,
Were going through a pinky spell.

When Dad collected her from school that day,
He asked what she told her classmates,
Of her hair dye accident, but she quickly said,
"Imagination is key within the school gates."

"I could have told the truth," Anna said,
"But that wouldn't have been fun,
It's better for them to think up fantastical things,
That they will believe since they're young."

Daddy agreed. "Adult life is boring,

There's not enough imagination about,
So let them believe what they want a little
longer,
They have the rest of their lives to doubt."

Teddy

Teddy had just had his third birthday,
He was growing up so fast,
He'd grown out of nappies and using a bottle,
And his dummy was the last.

As much as he wanted to be a big boy,
Teddy felt at a loss,
His dummy always made him feel better,
Whenever he felt tired or cross.

Mummy said he could give it to the dummy
fairy,
Hide it under his pillow for her,
She would come around and collect it one night,
But to keep it, he would prefer.

Teddy loved his dummy; his favourite thing,
He didn't want to let go,
He'd had a dummy since he was born,
But how else was he going to grow?

He thought it through and decided that day,
That he wanted to be a big boy,
He would give his dummy to his little brother,
This would surely bring Billy joy!

So that morning, he handed it over,
With a very heavy heart,
It took all his might not to cry,
But you see, Teddy was smart.

He had made a tough decision,
And unbeknownst to Mummy,
 When nobody was looking,
He could secretly suck his dummy.

He knew he had to grow up soon,
But why rush? He was only three!
So just for now, he'd try his luck,
And wean himself off slowly.

Olivia

It was Olivia's first parents evening,
Mummy and Daddy couldn't wait,
To see how well Liv was getting on,
When she was inside the school gate.

Olivia sat with her hands in her lap,
She really loved being at school,
She had lots of friends and loved to learn,
So she sat quietly on her stool.

Her teacher smiled and put on her glasses,
She reminded Liv of a mole,
The teacher sat up straight and said,
"She's a bossy little soul."

Mum and dad laughed. This they already knew,
She gave her big brother a run for his money,
"That's not a bad thing though," Dad chuckled,
"We think it's sort of funny."

Mrs Harris took her glasses back off,
"It can be good and bad.
It's good that she is asserting herself,
But can also make other children sad."

"Better to be bossy than be bossed around,"
Her mum truly believed,
"She just needs to find the right balance,
I'm sure this can be achieved."

Olivia was such a clever little girl,
She would often lead the flock,
The other children often looked to her,
When playtime came to knock.

But when they didn't want to play games,
Olivia would turn all red,
She'd stamp her feet and clench her fists,
And sit on her own instead.

"Sometimes we need to calm ourselves,
So we don't upset everyone,"
Mum gave Liv a cuddle then,
"You don't want to miss out on any fun."

"Next time try not to get angry,
It might help to count to ten,
Then play the game the others want to play,"
Daddy made lots of sense then.

Olivia didn't want to lose her friends,
So she decided to act more chill,
They could all have fun if they all played nicely,
And that was a pretty sweet deal.

Everlyn

"Today's the day!" Said Mummy proudly,
"We're going to trim those curls!"
But Everlyn said "No!" And pouted her lip,
She wanted long hair like other girls.

But Mummy told her it's only a little,
Just to give it some shape,
But Everlyn was still unsure,
And devised a plan to escape.

"It will only take a few minutes,
And if you're really good,
I'll treat you to an ice cream,
If you behave well like you should."

Everlyn was unconvinced,
She'd cut her finger before,
If someone was going to cut her hair,
They could hurt a lot more.

She screamed and cried all the way there,
Why would mummy cause her pain?
There was nothing wrong with her hair,
She loved her tangly mane.

Mummy calmly sat Everlyn down,
Right outside the door,
"You just have to sit very still,
And your hair will fall to the floor."

"It doesn't hurt, my darling girl,"
The hairdresser stroked her hair,
Then she snipped a tiny bit to show,
Everlyn didn't need to be scared.

Everlyn breathed a sigh of relief,
As her hair fell all around her,
She actually giggled at how silly she'd been,
She had caused quite a stir.

Mummy looked on, oh so proud,
A moment to treasure for sure,
And at the end, Everlyn got a gold star sticker,
She wanted to cut off some more.

But that was enough for her first hair cut,
It was no way as bad as it seemed,
And on their way home, Mummy kept her
promise,
Everlyn enjoyed her very own ice cream.

Beatrix

Beatrix was a fearless climber,
An explorer through and through,
And when her parents told her off,
Her curiosity grew.

She'd mastered the dining room table,
And climbed the stairs with ease,
She could make it onto the sofa,
Most of the furniture was a breeze.

But she still had yet to conquer,
Her biggest feat so far,
The kitchen counter top was high,
But it held the cookie jar.

Beatrix had figured a way to the top,
If she pulled out all the drawers,
She could make a stairway all the way,
And crawl up on all fours.

She'd almost made it, just one more step,
But then she wobbled and fell,
She smacked her arm on the tiled floor,
And let out a mighty yell.

Off to hospital, her parents drove,
She had broken her arm,
Mummy and daddy had warned her not to climb,
They knew it would cause her harm.

After a couple of months with her arm in a cast,
It was finally removed,
The doctor told her, "No more climbing!"
But Beatrix disapproved.

Within a few days, she devised a better plan,
And even though her parents were annoyed,
She didn't let a broken arm stop her,
From doing what she enjoyed.

Billy

"Excuse me," Billy pulled his Mummy's clothes,
He didn't want to be rude,
His mummy was talking to her friend,
But he really wanted some food.

He waited patiently for them to stop,
As he didn't want to annoy,
Then his Mummy's friend said,
"What a polite little boy!"

"Please may I have some lunch, Mum,"
Billy smiled and asked,
Mummy cuddled her little boy,
"Don't grow up too fast."

She handed him his sandwiches,
And patted him on the head,
"Thank you, Mummy. My favourite!"
Star shapes were cut into the bread.

His big brother Teddy demanded one too,
And Mummy put her hands on her hip,
"Why can't you be more like your brother?
He wouldn't give me any lip."

"Go to the naughty step, until you can be kind!"
Mummy had had enough,
Manners cost nothing is what they say,
So Mummy had to be tough.

Billy had very good manners,
Unlike his older bro,
But what Teddy didn't realise,
Is how far manners could go.

If Billy asked for something nicely,
It was more likely to be achieved,
It didn't hurt to be considerate,
And Mummy wouldn't get so peeved.

So manners go a long long way,
And help you even when you're old,
If you are nothing else, be kind,
And then you've really struck gold.

Jaxon

Jaxon was teaching Layla new tricks,
She already knew how to sit,
She could lay and beg and bark and heal,
But Jaxon wanted to try a new bit.

He held her treat high in the air,
And made a circle with his hand,
But Layla just stared and wagged her tail,
This wasn't what Jaxon had planned.

He wanted Layla to turn around,
Then jump to get her treat,
But Layla was not in the mood to learn,
She just wanted something to eat.

Jaxon was frustrated as Layla laid down,
She wasn't doing as she was told,
He wanted to show mum and dad what they'd
learnt,
Her other tricks were getting old.

Jaxon tried just one more time,
Drawing a circle again,
But Layla was so uninterested,
She was feeling really quite zen.

Jaxon was annoyed so he stomped his foot,
And sat beside his pup,
He gave her a stroke and tussled her fur,
And it was then that she stood up.

She waited calmly in position,
For Jaxon to voice his instruction,
And as he told her what to do,
She launched into her production.

She followed his hand, treat clenched in his fist,
She turned the whole way round,
Then at the end, she jumped up high,
And brought the treat down to the ground.

"What a good girl. You clever dog!"
Jaxon was very proud,
And mummy and daddy clapped their hands,
As Jaxon and Layla bowed.

"How did you teach her all these tricks?"
His parents were so impressed,
"All it takes is a little patience,
Then Layla does the rest."

Amirah

Two birthdays! Two Christmases!
Double the presents they swore,
Two houses! Two bedrooms!
But Amirah wanted it the way it was before.

She wanted her family together,
Her parents side by side,
She had been on her best behaviour,
In fact, she'd really tried.

She promised she would be a good girl,
Daddy wouldn't have to go,
But what she didn't realise was,
She was too young to know.

That sometimes grown-ups fall out of love,
Sometimes they grow apart,
They try and try to make things work,
But sometimes they need a fresh start.

And it's ok that they've changed their minds,
Because something will always be true,
The way Mummy and Daddy love Amirah,
Was more than she ever knew.

So, it is sad when Mummy's and Daddy's fight,
And sometimes it's horrible to see,
But sometimes parents need to split up,
In order to find their "Happy".

Just know that you are not the problem,
And it was never because of you,
If Mummy and Daddy can't work things out,
Then it's better to try something new.

This way, you get Mummy and Daddy all to
yourself,
You can spend quality time with them
Sometimes they're better parents apart,
Instead of together causing mayhem.

So just remember to cuddle them both,
And love them to your very core,
Because one things for certain when all's said
and done,
They have always loved you more.

Primrose

Primrose has dolly's and baby toys,
But her brothers don't want to play,
So she got oh so very excited,
When her friend came over one day.

They started playing together,
But then Primrose snatched her toys,
She upset her new little friend,
Who then made a wailing noise.

Mummy came in and sat Prim down,
"You must play nicely and share,"
But Primrose wanted all of her toys,
Why couldn't her friend bring a spare?

Mummy was angry and told Prim off,
She had to learn to share,
Her friend would not come round again,
And she'd have to sit on the naughty stair.

The next day, Primrose went to her friend's
house,
Her bedroom was so grand,
She had so many toys Prim had never seen,
So Prim reached out her hand.

Her friend handed Primrose her favourite toy,
And smiled as they started to play,
And Primrose realised it was much nicer,
Than it was the other day.

Maybe if she shared her own toys,
They could have even more fun,
If they each had a go and swapped things round,
Their games would be second to none.

So it's always best when you share with friends,
Imagine the fun to be had,
The adventures you'll go on and the games
you'll play,
See, sharing isn't really that bad.